Nai'a TO THE Rescue

STORY BY **Katie Grove-Velasquez** ILLUSTRATIONS BY **Michael Ogata**

MUTUAL PUBLISHING

For Tapani Vuori
who helped Nai'a get started on her adventures

Copyright © 2010 by Mutual Publishing

ISBN-10: 1-56647-930-4
ISBN-13: 978-1-56647-930-1

Third Printing, November 2012

Mutual Publishing, LLC
1215 Center Street, Suite 210
Honolulu, Hawai'i 96816
Ph: 808-732-1709 / Fax: 808-734-4094
email: info@mutualpublishing.com
www.mutualpublishing.com

Printed in Korea

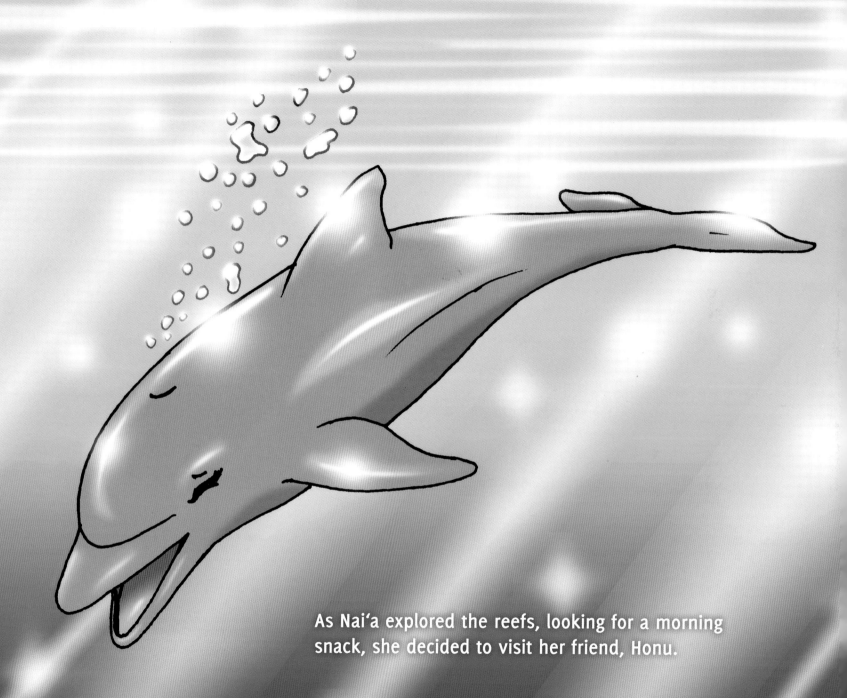

As Naiʻa explored the reefs, looking for a morning snack, she decided to visit her friend, Honu.

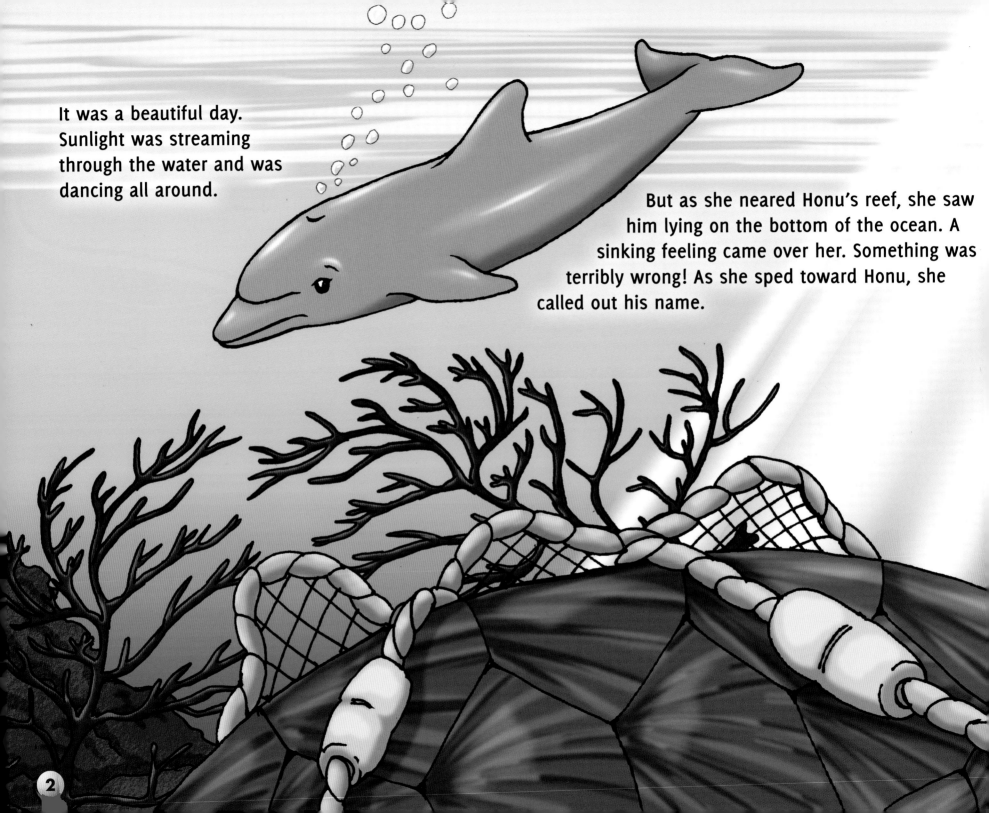

It was a beautiful day. Sunlight was streaming through the water and was dancing all around.

But as she neared Honu's reef, she saw him lying on the bottom of the ocean. A sinking feeling came over her. Something was terribly wrong! As she sped toward Honu, she called out his name.

"Honu! What is this?" asked Nai'a. She swam over to him, studying the strange object covering him.

Honu tried to raise his head, but he couldn't. He was trapped.

"Nai'a. This is terrible. This net fell on top of me while I was resting. It is very heavy, and I cannot move." Honu looked up at his friend's worried face. "Nai'a, you must help me. It has been a very long time since I've been to the surface."

Nai'a's heart pounded fast. If Honu couldn't move the net, Nai'a was certain she could not move it, either. She felt panic well up inside of her. Swimming circles over Honu, she saw that the net was very large.

Grabbing with her teeth, she pulled on the rope as hard as she could, trying to free him, but the net barely moved.

Honu hung his head and shook it slowly. "Nai'a you must hurry. Do something, anything, dear. I've been lying here, pondering this problem, but no answer comes to me. Think! Think! What should we do? I can't move, and I *must* get to the surface soon."

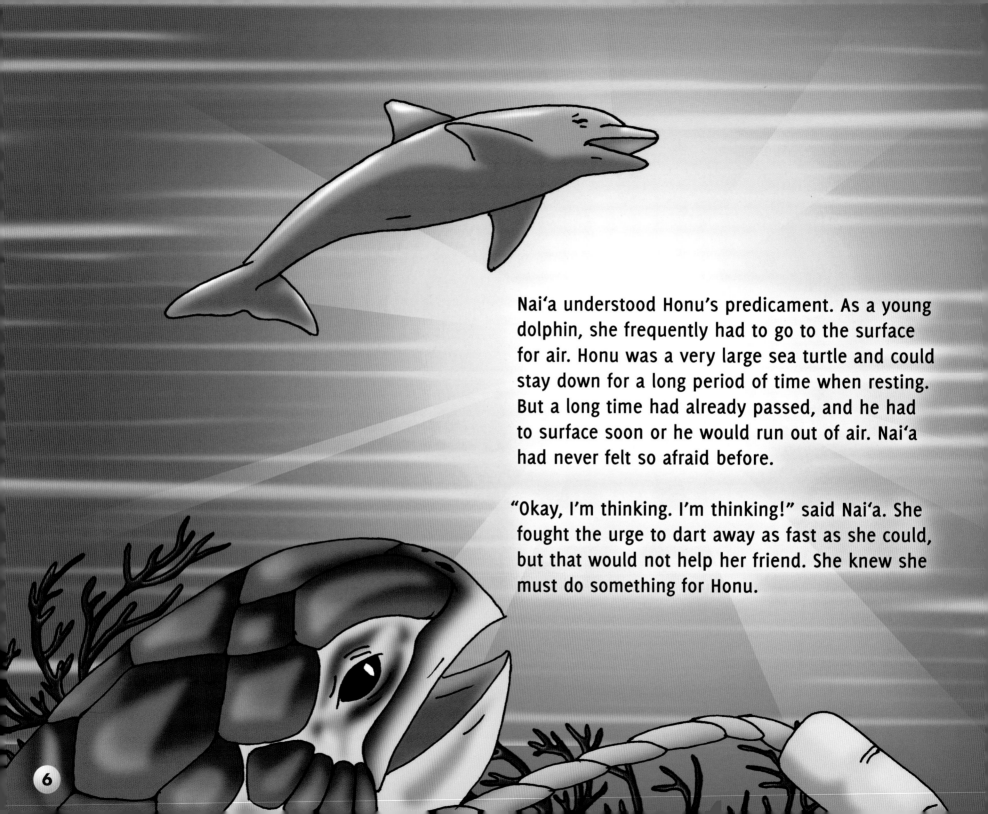

Nai'a understood Honu's predicament. As a young dolphin, she frequently had to go to the surface for air. Honu was a very large sea turtle and could stay down for a long period of time when resting. But a long time had already passed, and he had to surface soon or he would run out of air. Nai'a had never felt so afraid before.

"Okay, I'm thinking. I'm thinking!" said Nai'a. She fought the urge to dart away as fast as she could, but that would not help her friend. She knew she must do something for Honu.

She grabbed the net again and pulled with all her might, but it wouldn't budge. Her eyes filled with tears, as she swam to the other side of Honu and tried again.

"No, no no, my dear! Oh my dear Nai'a," Honu said softly. "Please don't waste your energy trying to move the net. Believe me, I've been trying to move under it for a long time, but I'm only getting weaker. I feel like the net is getting stronger. The more I struggle, the harder it is to move."

"Please allow me to help you," said a smooth and soft voice behind Nai'a.

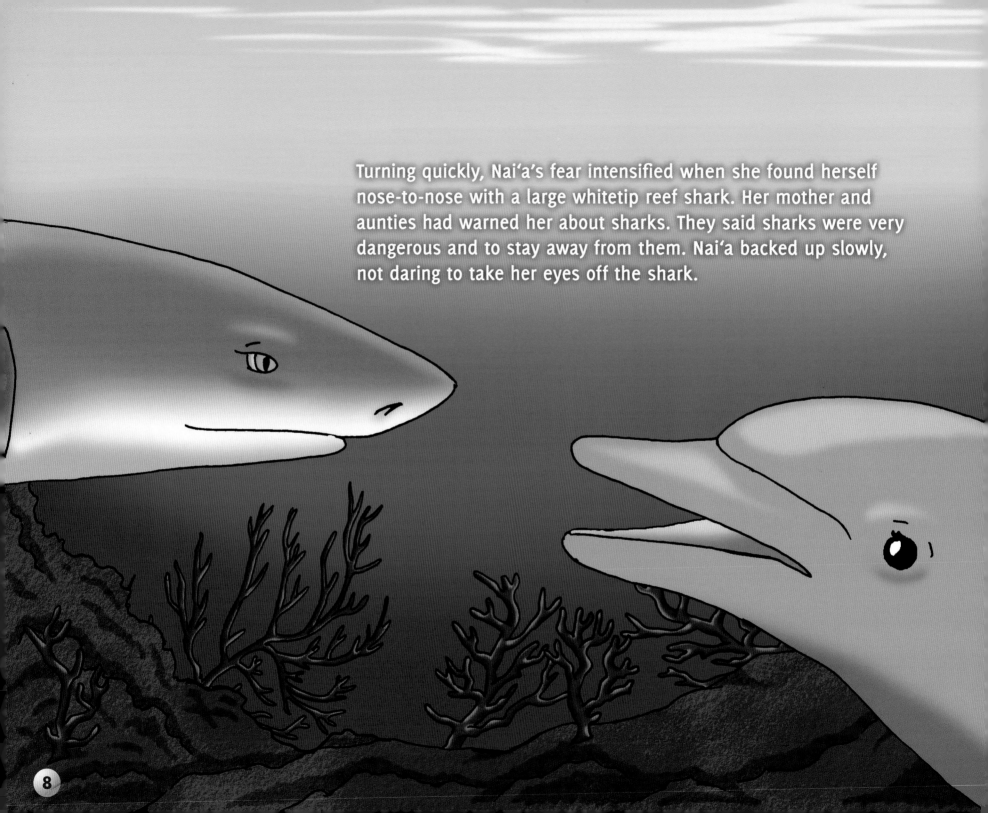

Turning quickly, Nai'a's fear intensified when she found herself nose-to-nose with a large whitetip reef shark. Her mother and aunties had warned her about sharks. They said sharks were very dangerous and to stay away from them. Nai'a backed up slowly, not daring to take her eyes off the shark.

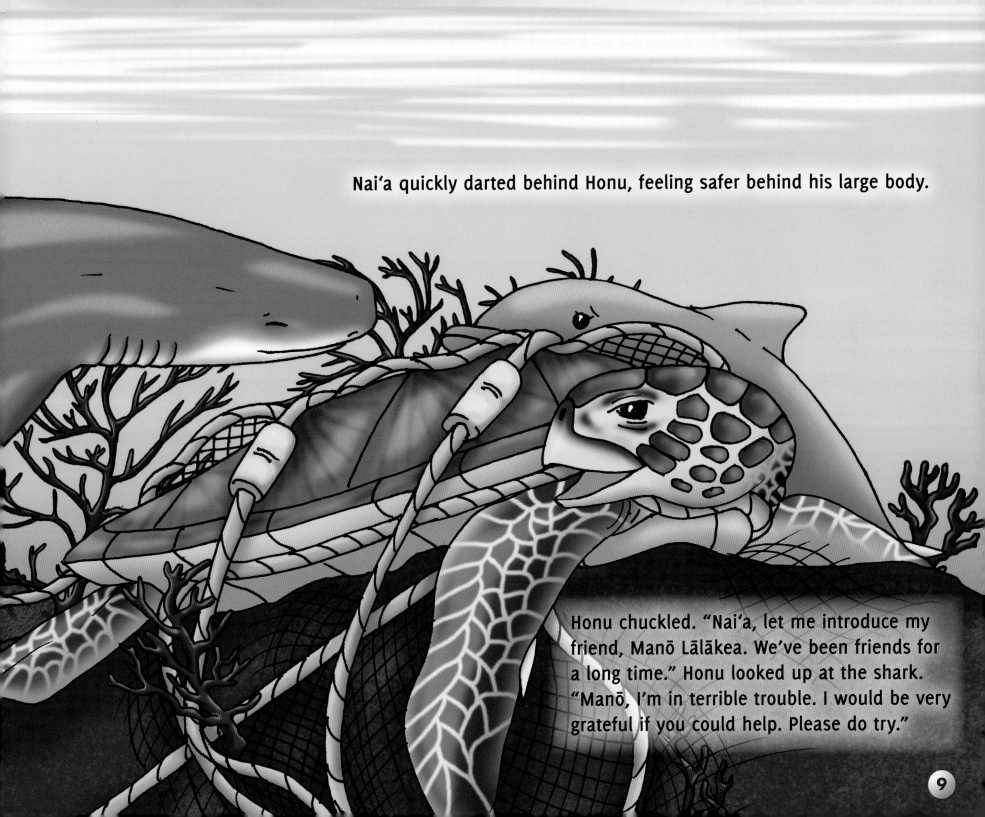

Nai'a quickly darted behind Honu, feeling safer behind his large body.

Honu chuckled. "Nai'a, let me introduce my friend, Manō Lālākea. We've been friends for a long time." Honu looked up at the shark. "Manō, I'm in terrible trouble. I would be very grateful if you could help. Please do try."

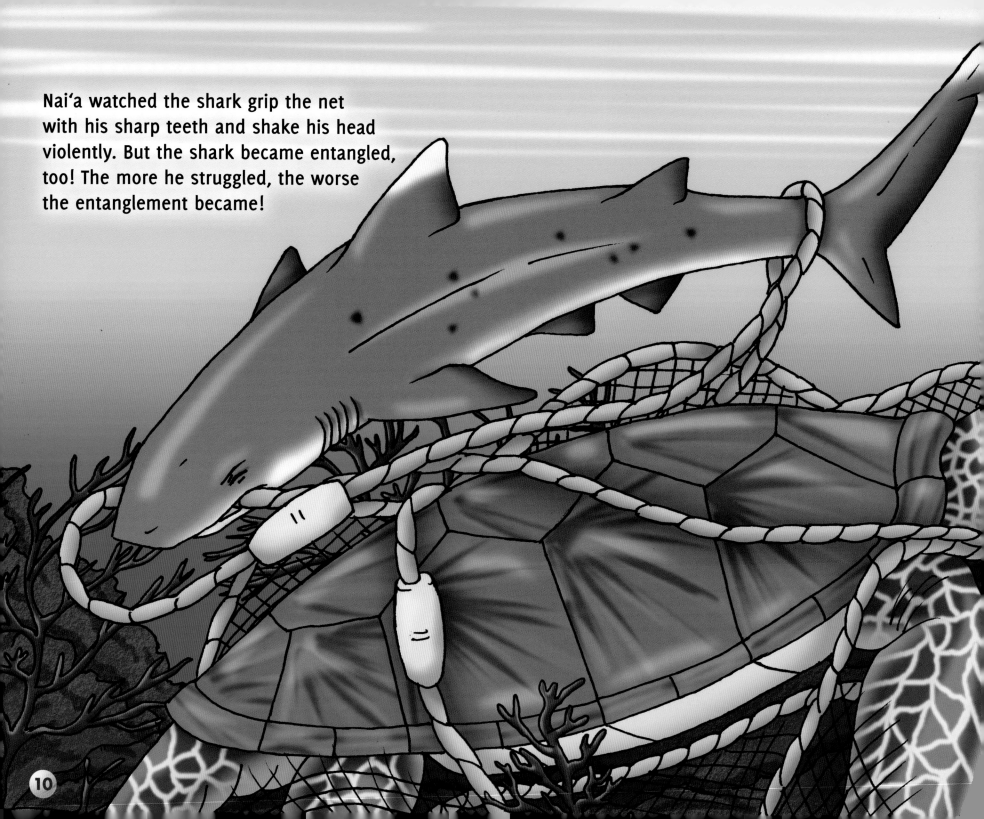

Nai'a watched the shark grip the net with his sharp teeth and shake his head violently. But the shark became entangled, too! The more he struggled, the worse the entanglement became!

Now Nai'a was more afraid than ever. She knew this could be the end for her friend if she didn't come up with a plan. Gazing down at Honu, she realized she needed air herself. Nai'a shot to the surface.

Taking several quick breaths, she swam in circles trying to think. She suddenly felt very angry at this predicament. NO! NO! NO! she thought. Honu must not die! I won't let him!

Leaping through the surface, she landed sideways with a tremendous splash. *There!* She felt a little better. *What is the answer?* she thought. Again and again she leapt out of the water and landed hard on the surface. *What is there to do?* Splash! *What can I do?* Splash! *I'm not strong enough!* Splash!

Then she remembered something her friend Koholā showed her when they had first met. She turned her head down in the water and slapped the surface with her tail over and over again. Slap! Slap! Slap! She hoped other friends would hear her and come to see what the trouble was. Maybe they could help her and Honu. Slap! Slap! Slap!

Nai'a swam down to tell Honu how she called for help and was surprised to see another friend trying to help. The Seven Eleven crab, 'Alakuma, was using his large, strong claws to cut through the net, but he was not making much progress. Nai'a murmured a quick thank you, as she swam to Honu. She placed her head against her friend's.

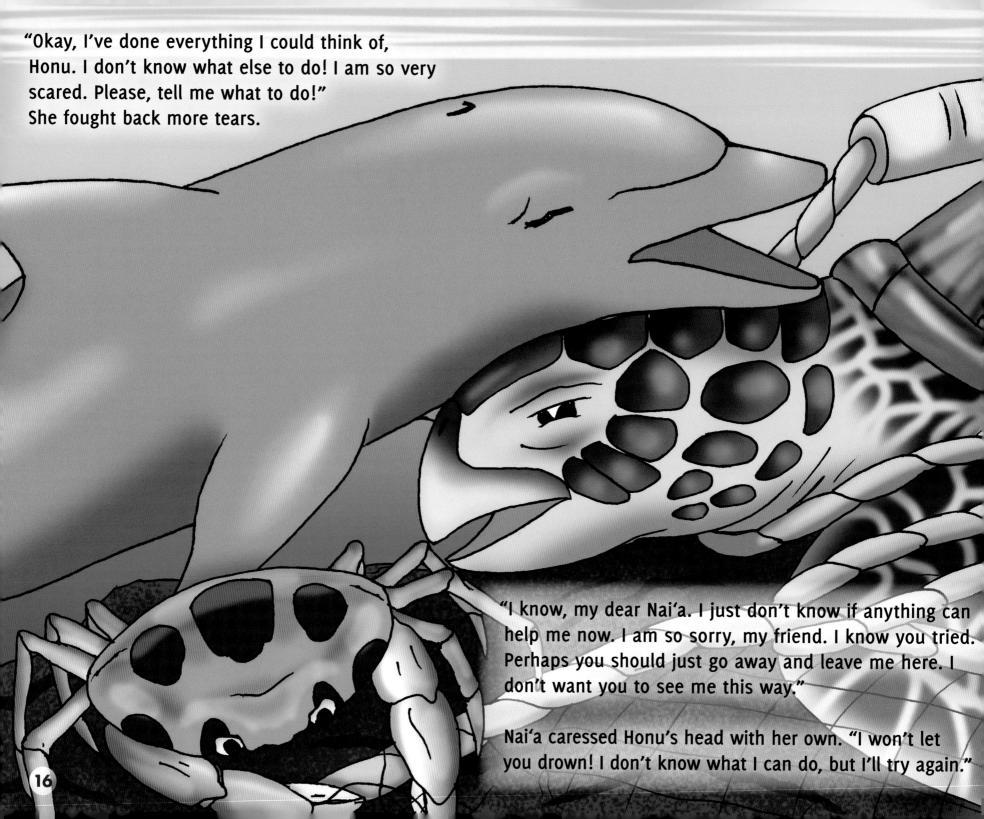

"Okay, I've done everything I could think of, Honu. I don't know what else to do! I am so very scared. Please, tell me what to do!"
She fought back more tears.

"I know, my dear Nai'a. I just don't know if anything can help me now. I am so sorry, my friend. I know you tried. Perhaps you should just go away and leave me here. I don't want you to see me this way."

Nai'a caressed Honu's head with her own. "I won't let you drown! I don't know what I can do, but I'll try again."

Quickly darting to the surface again, she leapt
out of the water as high as she could and twisted
her body hard, landing on the surface with a loud
smack! She tail slapped over and over.

Suddenly, she stopped and held very still. Nai'a heard a familiar sound. It was a motor, and she heard voices. The motor was very close, and the voices meant people! Her mother had told her that boats and people could be dangerous. Diving down, she told Honu about the boat.

"Bring the people closer," Honu urged.
"Maybe they will help us."

Nai'a saw another friend swimming over to help. It was Palani, a very large surgeonfish with a long, sharp spine at the base of his tail. With a nod of his head, he went to work, darting in and out of the net in an effort to cut the rope by Honu's head. Although he was not able to make much difference, Palani told Honu he would not give up.

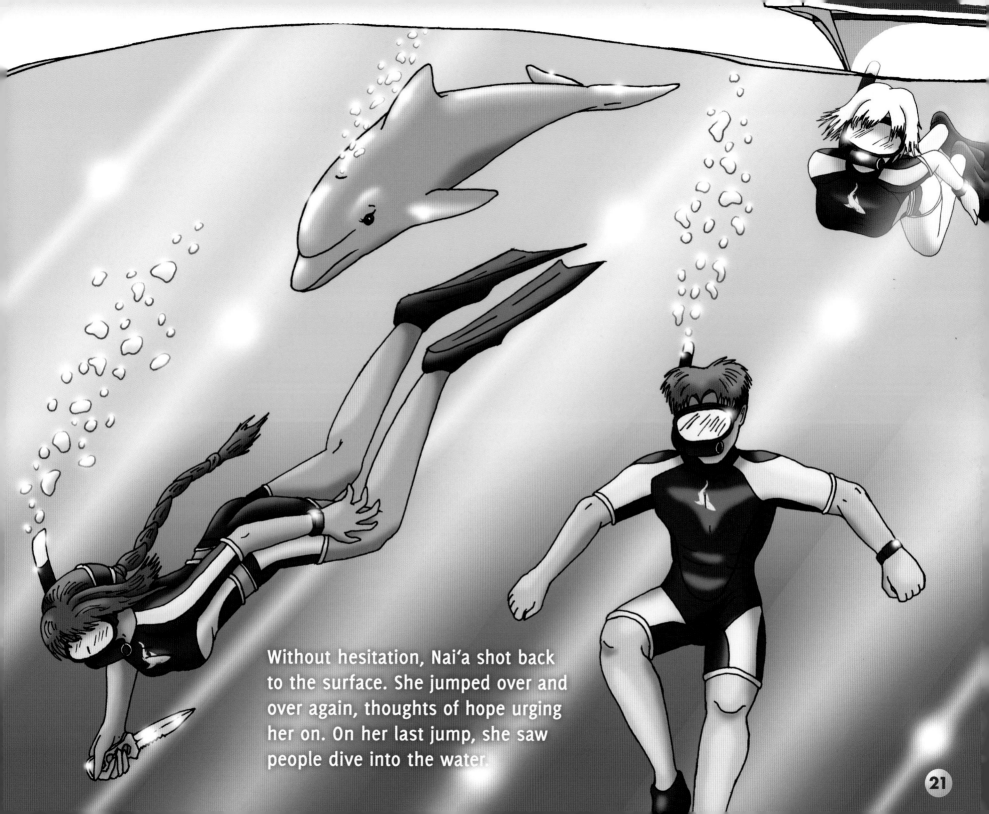

Without hesitation, Nai'a shot back to the surface. She jumped over and over again, thoughts of hope urging her on. On her last jump, she saw people dive into the water.

21

Swimming down to Honu, Nai'a saw people gathering around him, wearing strange masks. Some were pulling on the net. They were pulling very hard, but still, it would not move.

22

She watched one person holding something shiny swim down next to Honu. The person rubbed the shiny object against the net, and the rope broke away! Whatever this shiny thing was, it was cutting the net away from Honu's head.

One person freed Manō Lālākea, who whizzed by Honu. Soon, Honu was free! Naiʻa moved aside to give him room to swim to the surface. She followed anxiously behind him.

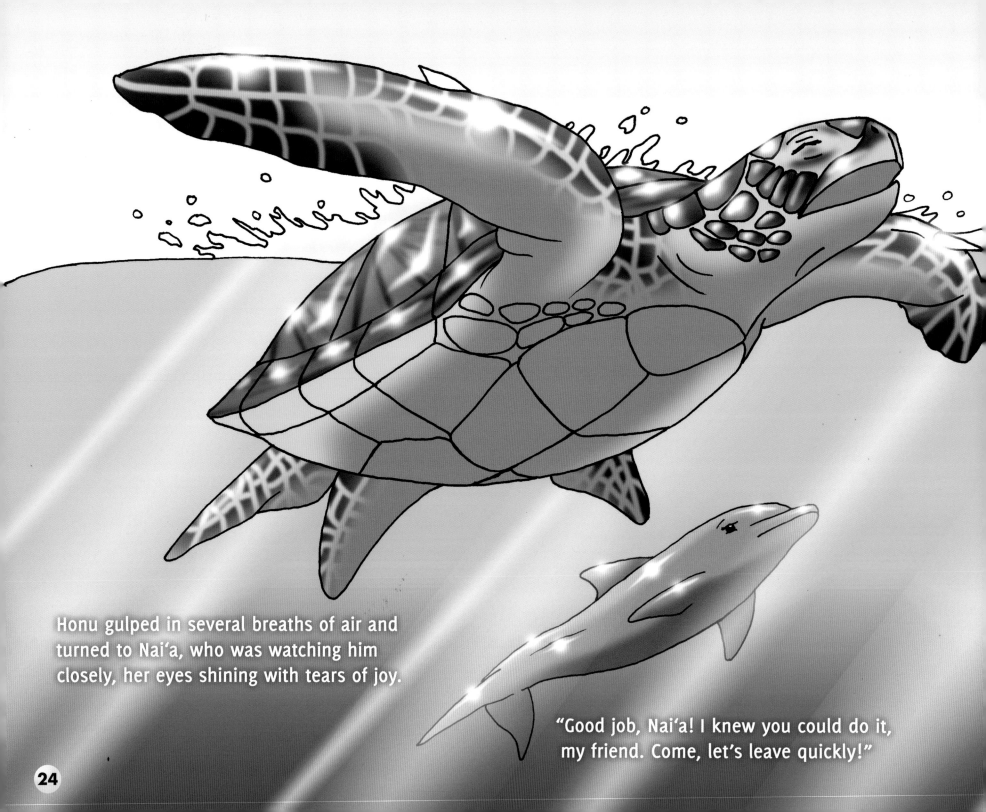

Honu gulped in several breaths of air and turned to Nai'a, who was watching him closely, her eyes shining with tears of joy.

"Good job, Nai'a! I knew you could do it, my friend. Come, let's leave quickly!"

As the shark approached, he shook his head slowly. "I'm so sorry Honu. I tried, really I did."

Honu nodded. "I know you did. I was more worried about you! Are you okay?"

The shark swam several slow circles before answering. "I am. See you soon. I am really happy to be able to say that!"

With a fast swish of his tail, he disappeared.

Honu and Nai'a swam a short distance away and dove down to watch the people as they ripped the net away from the coral reefs and gathered it up in large bundles. Diving again and again, they worked together to carry the bundles to the surface and place them on the boat. Soon they were gone.

Nai'a turned to Honu, her eyes large with fear. "Where did that net come from, Honu? Nets are so scary! You could have died!"

"I don't know, my dear, but thank you. Thank you so much for helping me."

"I didn't help! I wasn't strong enough. I really didn't do anything to free you," Nai'a insisted.

27

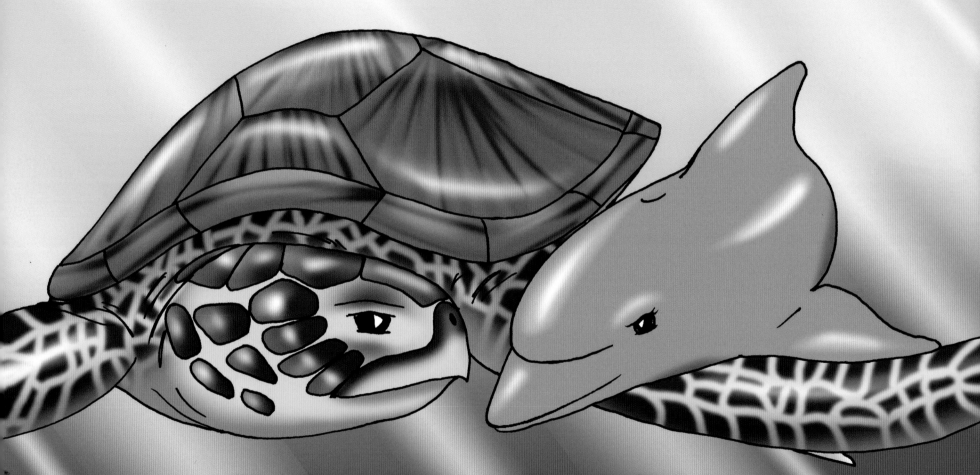

"Oh my dear, you did help, and so did our other friends. You brought those people to us so they could help. You saved me, Nai'a. You probably saved many other friends who could have been trapped as well." Honu said softly, looking deep into Nai'a's eyes.

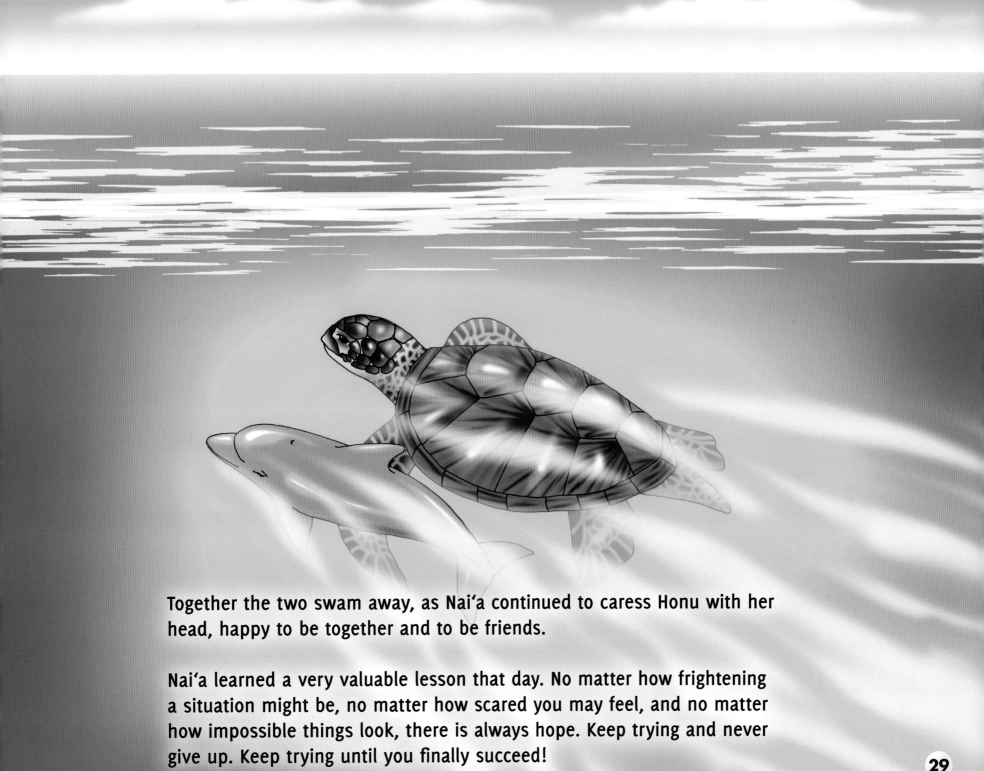

Together the two swam away, as Nai'a continued to caress Honu with her head, happy to be together and to be friends.

Nai'a learned a very valuable lesson that day. No matter how frightening a situation might be, no matter how scared you may feel, and no matter how impossible things look, there is always hope. Keep trying and never give up. Keep trying until you finally succeed!

Naiʻa's Friends of the Reef

Juvenile Oval Chromis

Lau wiliwili nukunuku ʻoiʻoi
Longnose Butterflyfish

Hā ʻukeʻuke kaupali
Helmet Urchin

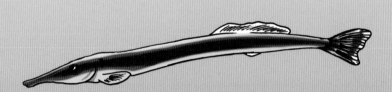

Bluestripe Pipefish

Commerson's Frogfish

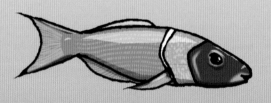

Hīnālea lauwili
Saddle Wrasse

Nai'a's Friends of the Reef

'Älo'ilo'i
Hawaiian Dascyllus

'Iwa
Frigate Bird

Mo'o lio
Yellow Seahorse

'Ū'ū
Big-scale Soldierfish

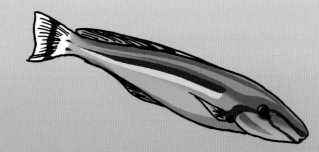

Smalltail Wrasse

Uhu uliuli
Spectacled Parrotfish

Nai'a's Friends of the Reef

Lupe
Broad Stingray

Lau'īpala
Yellow Tang

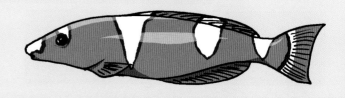

Hīnālea 'akilolo
Juvenile Yellowtail Coris

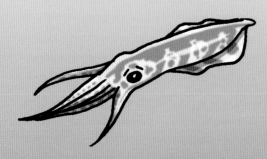

Mūhe'e
Oval Squid

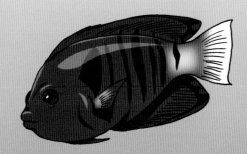

Flame Angelfish

'Ōkole emiemi
Sea Anemone

Nai'a's Friends of the Reef

'Alakuma
Seven Eleven Crab

Hawaiian Cleaner Wrasse

Hihimanu
Spotted Eagle Ray

Kūmū
Whitesaddle Goatfish

Aloalo
Mantis Shrimp

Hīnālea 'i'iwi
Bird Wrasse

Nai'a's Friends of the Reef

Humuhumunukunukuāpua'a
Reef Triggerfish

Hōkū kai
Knobby Star

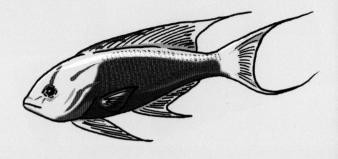

Hawaiian Longfin Anthias

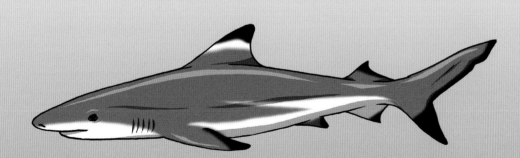

Manō pā'ele
Blacktip Reef Shark

Humuhumu'ele'ele
Black Durgon

Nai'a's Friends of the Reef

Manō kihikihi
Scalloped Hammerhead Shark

Puhi 'ōni'o
Whitemouth Moray Eel

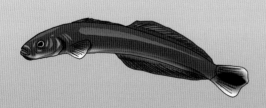

Spottail Dartfish

Kākū
Great Barracuda

Goldrim Surgeonfish

Nai'a's Friends of the Reef

Kihikihi
Moorish Idol

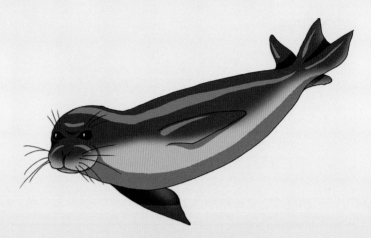

ʻĪlioholoikauaua
Hawaiian Monk Seal

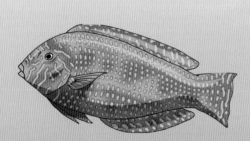

Shortnosed wrasse

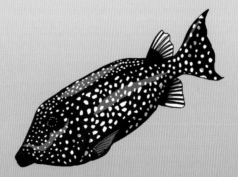

Moa
Spotted Boxfish

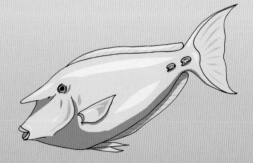

Kala
Bluespined Unicornfish

The End

ABOUT THE AUTHOR

Katie Grove-Velasquez is a marine naturalist, educator, lecturer, writer, diver, researcher, and amateur photographer who has been working and living in Hawai'i for over fifteen years. A mother of three grown children, Grove-Velasquez now spends most of her time working at a local aquarium, writing books and contributing to blog sites, and traveling with her husband of over twenty-one years.

ABOUT THE ILLUSTRATOR

Michael Ogata is a marine naturalist with a fondness for art and animations. A graduate of the University of Hawai'i at Mānoa, his particular field of interest is in sharks and their biology. Born and raised in Hawai'i, he has a passion for learning and educating people about the history, culture, and ecology of the islands. Ogata is also dedicated to the cause of environmental conservation.

Have you read about Nai'a's first adventure?

Join Nai'a on her birthday as she sets out with her mother to explore the reefs and their inhabitants. Anxious to make new friends, Nai'a meets a special animal who helps her learn the importance of acceptance and individuality and that the most important part of making a friend is to be a friend.

ISBN-10: 1-56647-912-6
ISBN-13: 978-1-56647-912-7

Trim size: 11 x 8.5 in.
Page count: 40 pp.

Hardcover
$14.95

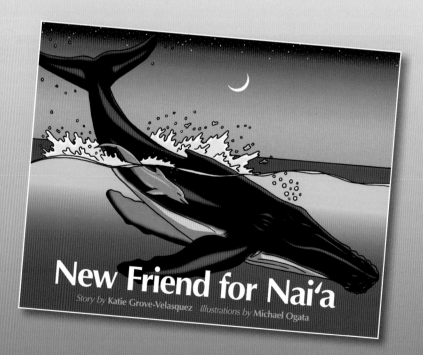

New Friend for Nai'a
Story by Katie Grove-Velasquez *Illustrations by* Michael Ogata